The
Rolling
Kitchen

The

Rolling

Kitchen

by

Ruth Patton Totten

RT Associates

2003

Second Printing

ISBN 0-9745791-0-6

Dedicated to the Ladies
of the Army Distaff Foundation

Contents

Let's Go South of the Border   23

Let's Take the Curse off Vegetables   36

Let's Have a Drink   43

Let's Travel — East of Gibraltar   52

Let's Have a Party

Wife and Mother Savers

Introduction

WHEN I was three years old my father came back from World War I, and we left the house of our Massachusetts grandparents for a thrilling new world. Our father was ordered to duty at Camp Meade, Maryland, with what was left of the Tank Corps. It was then a deserted and desolate wartime camp of tar-paper shacks and sand, but Mother, who had the heart of a pioneer woman, decided to move there and into anything she could find with a roof on it. We were given a 63-man barracks all to ourselves and she painted the whole of it blue and yellow inside, these being the Tank Corps colors and the only ones available at the post engineer's. My sister's room was blue with a yellow ceiling, and mine was yellow with blue. Mother planted oats in the sand for a lawn; we got a bull terrier pup named "Tank"; our playhouse was a real tank, in front of the chapel, and was famous for the number of German bullet holes in its rusty hide; there was an old retired soldier who had been scalped by Indians, who walked along the tracks in back of the house every evening (you could see the bare and shining scar on his head), and it was really living. There was only one problem: it didn't worry us but it bothered Mother. The barracks were tar-papered planks and the post commander ruled that there could be no cooking in these firetraps. I don't remember how she contrived, as we only ate once a day at the mess, another tar-paper palace, but we weren't hungry. However, I shall never forget the Sunday we were told that we were to be taken out on the firing range to have our dinner with the men — with the real soldiers!

"But how will they cook it? How will we eat?" my practical older sister kept asking, and was answered with the thrilling phrase: "You'll be fed from the rolling kitchens."

And then we saw them: the rolling kitchens, all lined up under a grove of locust trees, the horses that had pulled them there standing in a picket line behind them; the harness pole of each kitchen resting on a clean and open garbage can, smoke rising from each chimney, and the army cooks in clean white aprons, waiting for mess call.

We each got a tin plate, and there was canned corn (we had never tasted it before and it was ambrosial) and there was canned ham (ditto) and there was coleslaw, nice if you mixed it with the canned corn, and there was loads of hot bread (we never got it at home because it was Bad for Children) and there were canned peaches and squares of a kind of cake like the one Captain Hook cooked for the Lost Boys. There was never such food as came out of the rolling kitchens!

The soldiers called them the "slum guns" because they were mounted on the same sort of horse-drawn caisson as the artillery guns. Two horses to a kitchen, with a driver and a cook, they would lumber up with the baggage, behind the troops, to minister to the best-fed soldiers the world has ever known. Hats off to their redolent memory!

In a way, I have been driving a rolling kitchen for twenty-odd years, occasionally with a cook beside me. With a reluctant pause for World War II, we have kept up with our troops, and a genuine fondness for eating has made cooking part of the adventure. Our California grandmother told us that you had to know how to cook, even if you never had to, so that you could teach the cooks you could catch. I have been extremely lucky in knowing several cooks in several foreign lands who have caught and taught me. There was Goto, in Hawaii, who cooked classic rice and wrote three-line hokai that won prizes in the *Honolulu Advertiser*. There was little Rhoda, who cooked for Presidents, and occasionally chased her 200-pound consort around the kitchen with a cleaver — "and she means it, ma'am," said William as he puffed past. There was Rebecca, in Panama, who did miraculous deeds with elderly Panamanian fowl and rice and raisins, and whose grandmother had reportedly "come back" as a boa constrictor and strangled the goat of a neighbor she had hated. There was Elsie, who cooked fish better than anyone I have ever known but who found it hard to get around much, as her doctor had told her that her "pressure was so low that it scarcely got the blood above her knees."

The best cooking experience I ever had was cooking on a two-burner kerosene stove on fishing trips off the Perlas Islands in the Gulf of Panama, in the rolling seas. (That really was a rolling kitchen!) One of my most poignant memories is of a wild blue and white day with a "Wedgwood sky" when the huge bull dolphins, in their royal blue and yellow, were plunging in to snatch the bait from the grand Pacific sailfish we were trying to catch for the tournament (the dolphin were really just as much fun on the line, and they were edible, too). I had to fix a hot soup as we were tired and wet through and our redoubtable fishing friend, the British Minister, poked his head into the galley to inquire about the time and tenor of lunch.

I said, "We will have lunch in five minutes, and it's clam chowder."

He said, "Oh dear, do you suppose that I shall look down and see their sad little blue fringes waving at me?"

I still love clam chowder, but I *never* look down.

Then there was the two-burner on our little boat on the Potomac River, where we spent the summer weekends during tours in the Pentagon. After we passed Mount Vernon the water was clean, and we "crabbed" like mad till dark and then had "Crab-Any-Style," splendid with cold beer.

Our most advanced two-burner cooking was done while we moldered in a hotel in Izmir, Turkey, for six weeks while waiting for a house. There was one electric outlet in each of our two rooms, and as the electric current was whatever it is in Faraway Places, we had to buy two Turkish hot plates, which are simple and direct — either on or off, no compromise. Twice a day we served three-course meals, our thirteen-year-old daughter standing over the saucepan in the cell that she shared with her nine-year-old brother, and myself doing the fire-burn-and-cauldron-bubble on the other. Quite often lost souls wailed at our doors for the leftovers, having been fed at the officers' mess (five flights up and no elevator) and found it wanting.

But aside from cooking for cooking's own sake, it's cooking for the people that you meet while either fixing it, eating it, or talking about it that is fun. No matter where you are or who you are, the one thing that women can talk about, with no taboos broken, and no feelings hurt, is FOOD. This is a need and a hobby shared by all.

Of course, the farther you get from home, the more fearless you have to be, but usually the prize is worth the risk. (I quote a famous exception in our family, when Mother, from sheer politeness and an enthusiasm for ethnology, ate some raw dog's liver at a Hawaiian luau and just barely lived to regret it.) But keep your palate swinging free, and I promise you that a baby octopus, delicately fried in new olive oil, is delicious with Greek Ouzo (Turkish Raki), a licorice-flavored drink of power and tenderness. And raw Jerusalem artichokes are superb in a mixed green salad. And retsina, the turpentined Greek wine, leaves no hangover. And our favorite hors d'oeuvre, called Salmon Lomi in Hawaii and Seviche in Panama, is simply raw fish. What stories you can raise from these, and what memories!

In Turkey we lived between two Turkish doctors,

whose wives were famous cooks, one in the style of
Istanbul and the other in the style of Izmir. By use of
passwords, spies, and possibly tapping on the walls, each
knew when the other had brought us "a little something
to try." This deed would whip the other into a creative
frenzy that made our kitchen the spice market of the
Arabian Nights for two and a half years. Of course we
reciprocated in kind, and our various children and maids
were kept busy carrying loaded plates to the three
houses. For fear of seeming a braggart, no one sent much
of anything, only samples. Tobacco-flavored honey from
near ancient Colophon would inspire hot baking powder
biscuits; cheese-filled pastries would be acknowledged by
chocolate chip cookies. We barely spoke each other's
language, but we communicated in a deeper way. Good
cooks make wonderful friends. Somehow, through this
deeper bond, we exchanged recipes.

The precious gift that never grows old, never wears
out, and always brings a happy memory, is a favorite
recipe. The ones in our rolling kitchen are all gifts from
friends. Herewith I pass them on to friends. Keep 'em
rolling!

RUTH PATTON TOTTEN

Author's Note

THE FOLLOWING ingredients (not always found in every kitchen) are used in this book:

Foods

Roquefort cheese	Almonds	Cocoa
Parmesan cheese	Lentils	Cheddar cheese
Swiss cheese	American cheese	Candied ginger
Stuffed green olives	Bitter chocolate	"Bombay Duck"
Barley	Cream cheese	Mango chutney
Walnuts	Gelatin	Gruyère cheese
Pickled hot peppers	Pitted ripe olives	Cornstarch
Pistachio nuts	Cervelat	Honey
Hazelnuts	Yellow corn meal	Prunes

Canned Goods

Condensed cream of pea soup	Consommé	Salmon
Green turtle soup	Tomatoes	Corned beef
Beef bouillon	Tomato soup	Fricasseed chicken
Canned crabmeat	Canned chicken stock	Scotch broth
Canned mushrooms	Tomato paste	Kidney beans
Canned tuna fish	Mushroom soup	Pineapple rings
Canned hearts of artichokes	Canned whole chicken	Baked beans
Canned peas	Lobster	Chili beans

Seasonings

Cayenne pepper	Prepared mustard	Horseradish, prepared
Chili powder	Tabasco	
Dry mustard	Curry powder	

Herbs and Spices

Nutmeg
Thyme
Bay leaf
Cloves, whole and
  ground
Tarragon
Peppercorns
Coriander, ground
Cumin seed
Orégano

Mace
Mustard seed
Celery salt
Paprika
Dill weed
Sage
Dried mint
Cinnamon, whole
  and ground
Sweet basil

Dried parsley
Dried basil
Dried rosemary
Green tea
Ground allspice
Dried summer
  savory

Liquors and Liquids

Mushroom sauce
Dark rum
Olive oil
Sherry (table) or
  cooking sherry
Port
Cognac
Worcestershire
  sauce
Curaçao
Vanilla extract
Bourbon whiskey
Mint extract
Vinegar

Catsup
Crème de Menthe
Sour cream
A–1 sauce
Angostura bitters
Falernum
Rosewater
Almond extract
Kirsch
Soy sauce
Peach brandy
Grape juice
Gold rum
White rum

Gin
Rye whiskey
Claret
Benedictine
Sauterne
Moselle
Champagne
Rhine wine
Cointreau
Apricot liqueur
Ginger beer
Cider

In every recipe calling for butter, oleomargarine can, of
course, be used. It just takes so long to write it out.

The
Rolling
Kitchen

Let's Visit
the Hall of Fame

THERE ONCE WAS a famous Field Artilleryman, back between the two world wars, named "Toddy" George. He was a masterful horseman, and a great horse-show rider, and he was very quick-tempered. He was married to a wonderful woman — when Toddy was fire, she was snow; when Toddy was poisonous, she was bland; they were each other's complement in every way. Her father was the Vice-president of the United States, but she never tried to be anything but Mrs. Toddy George. And — she had A Secret. When the word got around that

Toddy was in a bad temper, someone would inform "Perm" — he would come home to —

Mrs. George Washington's Crab Soup

FOR FOUR:

- 2 hard-boiled eggs
- 1 tablespoon butter
- 1 tablespoon flour
- 1 quart milk
- 1½ cups crabmeat, picked over carefully
- ½ cup cream
- ⅛ cup sherry (or more, to taste)
- Salt and pepper
- Nutmeg
- ½ teaspoon mushroom sauce (Cross and Blackwell: optional)

Mash eggs to a paste with a fork, and add to them the butter, flour and pepper. Bring milk to a boil and pour it slowly onto the egg paste.

Put over a low fire, add crabmeat and simmer 5 minutes. Add cream, bring to the boiling point again, and add sherry, salt, pepper, nutmeg and sauce. Keep hot over boiling water.

I like to think of the Father of His Country and the Commanding Officer of an Artillery Post both going back to the petty harassments of ruling men in a good disposition. (This also works on cavalrymen, infantrymen, and aviators.)

They have kept this pot boiling lo, these many years, and who knows, perhaps this is the secret behind the power to filibuster!

United States Senate Bean Soup

FOR EIGHT:

Take 2 pounds small white navy beans, wash, and run through hot water until the beans are white again. Put over a medium fire with 4 quarts of hot water.

Boil with 1½ pounds smoked ham hocks, slowly for 3 hours, in just enough water to cover, in a covered pot. Braise 1 large onion, chopped, in a little butter, and add to soup when light brown. Season with salt and pepper, and serve.

A nice touch for a winter day is to mash one hard-boiled egg to a paste in the bottom of each soup bowl, and pour on about 2 tablespoons of sherry before adding the soup.

To keep the endearing curves that won her Diamond Jim and also Judge Bean, the "law West of the Pecos," Miss Lillian Russell had recourse to this hotbed of calories — but oh! what an easy way to live!

Lillian Russell

FOR SIX:

- 1 can condensed cream of green pea soup
- 1 can water
- 1 can green turtle soup
- 2 or more tablespoonsful of sherry
- 1 cup whipped cream, salted

Bring all liquids to the boiling point, add sherry, and pour into ovenproof serving bowls. Top each bowl with whipped cream and brown under the broiler for 1 minute.

The Duchess of Windsor has given us a lot to talk about down the years, including the pleasing fact that a woman of forty is still a femme fatale. However, one of the best conversational starters she has provided is the following eye-opener of a meal-opener.

The Duchess of Windsor's Avocado Cocktail

Cream Roquefort cheese with half its weight of cream cheese, add rum until it is the consistency of soft butter, add a touch of scraped onion, a dash of lemon juice, and fill the hollows in halved, pitted avocados. Half an avocado per person.

Antoine of New Orleans contributes this perfect brunch, or ladies' luncheon dish, which takes the curse off two of the plainer vegetables and renders them into a memory.

Spinach Florentine with Eggplant

Arrange a bed of cooked, buttered spinach in the bottom of a large, shallow casserole. Cover it with very thin slices of eggplant that have been peeled and sautéed in butter. Cover the eggplant with Mornay Sauce and brown under the broiler. One box of spinach for three people.

Mornay Sauce:

Make a cream sauce with 2 tablespoons each of flour and butter to one cup of milk. Add slowly 2 tablespoons butter, and 2 tablespoons each of grated Parmesan and grated Swiss cheese, with cayenne to taste.

A more fanciful version of this is to cover the eggplant slices with very lightly poached eggs and then add the *Sauce Mornay*. Oh! for a cold Sunday night!

In the time of Tamerlaine, the Great, there was a holy man, or Hodja, in Turkey called Nas'r'din Hoja. He was a real Foxy Grandpa, and is still beloved by Turkish children, and by the American children who have read of him and have laughed at his antics. He was always off teaching and talking, and his wife was an inveterate gossip and never had the meals on time. They were very poor, because Nas'r'din Hoja was always giving his last coin to someone less fortunate. One day his wife was so entranced with the scandal being discussed at the well that she put off going home till the last minute and then she ran all the way home, and without stopping to catch her breath, simply threw together her husband's favorite stuffed eggplant. The story has two endings — the Hoja came in and saw how much olive oil she was putting into the dish: or, the Hoja liked it so much he ate the whole thing — but the finale is the same.

The Priest Fainted (*Imam Bayeldi*)

FOR EIGHT:

5 medium onions, sliced very thin
3 large tomatoes, peeled and chopped fine
1 clove minced garlic
1 bunch parsley, chopped fine
Salt and pepper
4 medium eggplants
1 cup olive oil
2½ cups water
1 tablespoon sugar

Put onions, tomatoes, garlic and parsley in a bowl with ½ teaspoon salt, pepper to taste. Peel eggplants so that they are striped, one strip peeled, the next unpeeled. Slash them on one side and stuff the slashes with the other mixture. Arrange side by side in a casserole, add oil, 2½ cups water, sugar and add salt to taste. Cover tightly and cook in a moderate oven about 1½ hours.

A nice version of this is to add ½ to 1 pound of hamburger to the stuffing.

President Eisenhower is a very talented man, and has certainly eaten "higher on the hog" than most of us, but the great Queen of Sheba "talked to the butterflies when e'er she walked abroad," as Kipling tells us, and the President of the U.S.A. has not forgotten that some of the simplest things are best.

President Eisenhower's Old-Fashioned Beef Stew

FOR SIX:

Heat 4 tablespoons fat. Add 2 pounds round of beef, cut into 1½-inch cubes. Brown. Add 2 peppercorns, 1 bay leaf, 3 cloves, ½ teaspoon thyme, pinch of cayenne, 1 garlic clove, halved; 3 cans beef bouillon. Cover and simmer 1 hour. Add 1 pound small peeled Irish potatoes, 1 bunch carrots, cubed; 8 to 10 small onions; 2 tomatoes, chopped. Simmer uncovered 40 minutes, or until the vegetables are tender. Remove spices. Combine 3 tablespoons each of flour, water and stew stock; blend, add to stew and stir until thick.

Esau sold his birthright for a "Mess of Pottage." He had had a hard life, right from the beginning — and it really was right around the beginning, at least, of known history. This recipe is traditional — it should go on the same page with the pudding Mrs. Noah made out of all the leftovers on the Ark! In fact, it will!

Esau's Pottage

FOR THREE OR FOUR:

1 cup lentils
1 large onion, sliced
½ tablespoon of butter
1 pound of lamb, cubed
Salt and pepper
1 cup rice
2 cups water

Wash the lentils, soak overnight in 2 quarts of water, and drain. Brown the onion in butter and add to the lentils. Add meat, water to cover, salt and pepper. Cook slowly. When the lentils are almost tender, add rice, 2 cups of water, and simmer, stirring occasionally, until rice is cooked.

Noah's Pudding

FOR SIX:

¼ pound chick peas
¼ pound lima beans
1 pound barley
1 ounce butter
2 ounces chopped figs
2 ounces raisins
2 pounds sugar
1 cup milk
1 tablespoon rose water
5 ounces pistachio nuts
5 ounces chopped hazelnuts
5 ounces almonds
5 ounces walnuts
Pomegranate pulp

Soak peas and beans overnight. Cook barley in water till tender. Strain, change water, strain again. Mash ½ of barley through a sieve and add ½ the butter. Add the beans, peas, figs, raisins, sugar and milk to the unstrained barley in the pan. Cook 10 minutes and add the strained barley. Flavor with rose water and cook about 2 hours, until it is like custard. Turn into a bowl, chill and serve decorated with nuts and pulp.

As a matter of fact, though unorthodox, this is perfectly delicious and very nourishing. It tastes like a very unusual custard, and no one can ever tell what is in it.

When Major George Smith Patton, Jr., came back from station in Hawaii in 1928 and arrived for duty in Washington, Mrs. Patton went to look for a cook. Her eye was caught and held by a tiny little white-haired woman, not quite five feet tall, who looked as if a strong breeze would whirl her away. Although Mrs. Patton had in mind something a good deal bigger and stronger to feed her ravening family, instinct prevailed over inclination, and Rhoda was installed for seven Lucullan years. When she produced her first magic platter, saying in a soft Yorkshire voice, "This was the President's favorite snack," Major Patton said, "Which President?" and Rhoda replied, "Him that you called Teddy Roosevelt, sir. I cooked for they for many good years." When asked why this had not been mentioned at the interview, she answered, "Tha never aksed me, maam."

President Theodore Roosevelt's Favorite Snack

(also marvelous for brunch, midnight suppers, and sudden guests)

FOR THREE:

6 well-beaten eggs
3 tablespoons cream
1 tablespoon Worcestershire sauce
Salt, pepper, cayenne to taste
Butter
6 tablespoons grated American cheese

Mix eggs, cream and Worcestershire sauce with egg-beater; season with salt, pepper, cayenne and allow to sit at least 15 minutes. Melt plenty of butter in a skillet, allowing enough to pour onto 3 slices of toast, and leaving about 2 tablespoonsful in the skillet. Stir the cheese into the egg mixture and scramble until thick but not rubbery. *Serve at once.*

Professor Agassiz, of Harvard University, was one of the truly great naturalists of all time. He was charming and a bon vivant as well, and his granddaughter produces this dream of simplicity for those of us who like to "cook the party the day before."

Anna Prince's Pots de Crème au Chocolat

FOR SIX:

3 eggs
½ cup sugar
2 squares bitter chocolate
½ teaspoon vanilla extract

Beat the eggs separately. Add the sugar to the beaten yolks and beat well. Melt the chocolate over hot water and beat again into the yolks and sugar. Fold in the vanilla and the stiffly beaten whites, pour into 6 small cups. Chill, and serve with whipped cream.

Any good liqueur can be substituted for the vanilla and give a rare and exotic taste. This has been a favorite every time it was ever served.

Catherine the Great, Catherine the Great: she looked so well in the things she ate! But that was much, much later when she was old and fat and raddled. When she was young and svelte and amorous, this was what she had to offer — that is, one of many things she had to offer! It is a wonderful party dessert, particularly since they have invented the squeeze-bottle whipped cream.

Strawberries à la Czarina

FOR FOUR OR FIVE:

Stem 2 cups of berries, powder with confectioners' sugar, and chill in the serving dish. Blend 2 tablespoons each of port, Curaçao and cognac, and pour over the berries. Cover with whipped cream, flavored with curaçao, and serve.

Let's Call on Some
Old Soldiers

OLD SOLDIERS have been kept from fading away for years and years and years by these following standbys of army life:

Julie Totten's Scrambled Eggs

FOR TWO:

½ cake Philadelphia cream cheese
½ cup cream
4 eggs well-beaten
Salt, pepper, chopped chives

Melt cream cheese in the cream, stir eggs into the hot mixture, season and scramble till velvety.

These are fine for Sunday breakfast, or lunch, or after the football game.

ꝏꝏ

One of the most distinguished military families of the Army is the De-Russy-Hoyle-Herr-Holbrook-Murray-Stanley-Rumbough clan; they are also best-beloved, and on top of all that, their hospitality is fabulous and famous. When Ruth Ellen Patton married Jim Totten, her mother's friends gave her a "Recipe Shower" and a lot of well-kept family secrets came to light, and one of the best of all is —

Mrs. John Herr's Seafood Newburgh

FOR SIX:

2½ cups rich cream sauce
2 egg yolks, well beaten
3 cups cooked seafood
2 tablespoons butter
4 tablespoons sherry
Salt and cayenne

When the cream sauce has reached the boiling point, remove from the fire and slowly blend in the egg yolks. Add seafood, butter, sherry and seasoning. Do not boil again, but keep hot over hot water.

This is far superior to the traditional newburgh as it will keep for hours, never curdles, and always tastes delicious.

About 1940 a brand-new bride arrived at Fort Sill, Oklahoma, with a complete set of cooking utensils, Fannie Farmer's Cook Book, and the sum total of her knowledge of housekeeping was how to make a bed, make fudge, and make waffles. Her mother had been a notable hostess, so she knew what she wanted, but she didn't know how to produce it. However, the time came for her husband's birthday party and she optimistically asked thirty people and set out with Fannie Farmer and grim determination to achieve something "like Mother used to make." The eggs were boiling, the ham was boiling, the mixes were half mixed, the floor was half polished, the silver was half polished, and the bride was boiling and completely un-polished, when there was a soft knock at the door and a black and smiling face looked in, then a gentle voice said, "Honey, you sure does need a maid about as bad as I ever seen." Among the many things contributed to that first year of marriage by the wife of Sergeant Bolton was —

Margaret Bolton's Stuffed Eggplant

FOR FOUR:

1 large eggplant
Olive oil
1 grated onion
1 cup bread crumbs
1½, or less, pounds ground meat
Salt, pepper, butter
2 or more tablespoons of chili powder
1 egg, well beaten

Cut the top off the eggplant and scoop out the pulp, leav-ing the shell about ½ inch thick. Chop the pulp and cook in a little olive oil until it is transparent. Add onion. Cool. Add crumbs, meat, seasoning and egg and mix well. Fill eggplant with mixture and bake in the oven at 350° for about 45 minutes. This is fine for any meal, and lovely on a buffet table.

While old soldiers are lying and bragging to each other about how wet it was on the last maneuvers, or how hot, or how fouled up, their good ladies are apt to be comparing notes on friends, family, and food. Connie Booth produced this superb party dish at Fort Benning, and gave it to a friend as a going-away present. It is one that has been treasured for many years. One nice thing about that kind of going-away present is that no matter how many times you use it, it never wears out!

Connie Booth's Crabmeat and Mushrooms in Wine

FOR FIVE:

1 pound fresh backfin crabmeat or 2 8-oz cans
¼ lb fresh mushrooms or 1 8-oz. can
2 tablespoons butter
2 tablespoons flour
½ cup milk
½ cup white wine or sherry
½ teaspoon dry mustard
¼ teaspoon dry tarragon
Salt and pepper
Herb-seasoned crumbs

Pick over the crabmeat. Slice and sauté the mushrooms in some butter. Make a cream sauce with the other ingredients, add crabmeat and mushrooms, place in a casserole, cover with crumbs, dot with butter and bake at 350° for 30 minutes.

There was once a four-star General who would not eat fish. His wife, being from New England, was very fond of fish and felt that the children should learn to eat everything. However, the General said that the smell of fish cooking made him sick, that the taste of it made him sicker, and that the thought of dead fish in the icebox, looking at him with their sad little eyes, broke his heart.

He said it when he was a second lieutenant, and he kept right on saying it until he was gathered to his reward and could say it no more. He never guessed that his favorite chicken casserole was —

Tuna Temptation

FOR FIVE:

1 can tuna fish
1 can of hearts of artichokes
1 small can button mushrooms
Salt, pepper, dash of dry mustard
2 cups cheese sauce

Wash the tuna in a strainer, under hot water, till all the oil is gone, and drain well. Place ingredients in a casserole, in layers, and cover with cheese sauce. Heat until brown and bubbly.

The mess sergeant of Dog Battery of the 349th Field Artillery was a wise old man. He couldn't read or write very well, but he wore glasses, which gave him a very educated look. His hot rolls were certainly the result of an educated taste, and he could turn them out in a field kitchen as well as in barracks. He didn't need an oven thermometer, he could tell the temperature of his oven by holding his hand inside and counting slowly. A "number 10 oven" was medium, and a "number 3 oven" was very hot. He also produced this delectable luncheon dish:

Green Rice

FOR FIVE:

- 2 eggs, beaten separately
- 1 cup boiled rice
- 3 onions, grated
- 1 cup rat cheese, grated
- 3 tablespoons olive oil
- 2 green peppers, grated
- ½ cup chopped parsley
- ¾ cup milk
- Salt and pepper

Beat the egg whites till stiff. Mix other ingredients, including beaten yolks, in a casserole, fold in the whites, set the casserole in a bowl of water and bake 45 minutes in a "number 10 oven" (350° for those of us with tender hands).

General George S. Patton, Jr., was not one to lurk around the kitchen and bother the cook. He was the "autocrat" of not only the breakfast table, but any meal table. However, he was a fine shot and loved to hunt, and very few cooks can handle game. They tend to overcook it, or overclean it, or generally try to treat it like Spam. These two recipes for game were his very own, but whether he invented them or borrowed them or inherited them, history does not relate. However, they are both worthy.

Georgie's Doves

TWO DOVES APIECE:

Doves
Butter
Garlic salt
Canned beef bouillon
Carrots, cut small
Celery, chopped
Onions, chopped
Mushrooms, canned or fresh, drained
Peas, canned or fresh, drained
Pepper, salt, flour

Use the breasts of the doves only, simply cut away the other parts and leave the breasts whole, like little boats. Skin, and brown in butter, flavoring them with garlic salt. Save the butter in the skillet. Put bouillon, carrots, celery, onion, mushrooms, peas and seasonings in a deep pan. Add breasts, and simmer 1 hour. (He said 2 hours but I prefer 1 hour.) Add flour to fat in skillet and make gravy with the stock from the doves. Serve the doves swimming in gravy, with toast.

Georgie's Quail in Duffel Coat

ONE QUAIL APIECE:

Clean a quail, or any small game bird, put a lump of butter inside of it. Sprinkle with salt, pepper and garlic salt. Cut a large Idaho potato in two and scoop out enough of each side to make a hollow for the bird. Tie the potato together tightly with string and bake 1 hour at 450°.

Sunday night suppers among the Southerners in the regular army ran along these lines: kidney stew on waffles, salad, and a big chocolate cake. Waffles now come in a mix and so does chocolate cake, but no mix can ever duplicate the Colonel's wife's kidney stew. It was like peanuts — more-ish.

Confederate Kidney Stew

THREE KIDNEYS APIECE (IF THEY ARE LAMB KIDNEYS, ONE APIECE IF THEY ARE BEEF KIDNEYS):

Kidneys, lamb if possible
Grated onion to taste
Sliced mushrooms, fresh or canned
Butter, salt, pepper, flour
Canned consommé
Sherry

Parboil the kidneys and set aside. When cool, remove the white membrane. Sauté the onion and mushrooms in butter. Cut the kidneys very fine, and add to the sautéeing mushrooms. Add consommé and cook until almost done, thicken the gravy with flour, and flavor with sherry to taste just before serving.

This recipe is the astonishing result of the efforts of an officer's wife stationed at Fort Clark, Texas, back in the Indian-fighting days, who wanted to make a Charlotte Russe to impress the visiting Inspector General, and did not have any of the right ingredients. To say that the IG was impressed is an understatement. Fort Clark isn't a Fort any more, it's a resort; but in the graveyard among the many, many headstones marked "Unknown Civilian," there is one last reminder of the Bad Old Days; it is a headstone with this inscription:

Oh! Stranger, remember to pray for the soldier
Who rode o'er the ranges for many a year;
He chased the Comanches away from your ranches,
And harried them far o'er the distant frontier.

Well, let the following dessert be a happy memory among the grimmer one of border days.

Bourbon Crème

FOR FOUR:

Lady fingers
1 pint heavy cream
1 tablespoon gelatine
½ cup hot water
½ cup sugar
½ cup (or more) bourbon whiskey

Line a mold with lady fingers. Whip the cream; dissolve the gelatin in the hot water, cool, and add to cream. Add sugar, whiskey, and chill till firm.

Mrs. George S. Patton, Jr., didn't learn to cook until she was nearly forty. Then "Georgie" decided to sail to his next station in Hawaii in his schooner, the *Arcturus*. He believed in testing his luck, because he said one had to be lucky to be promoted in peacetime, and he didn't want to be a Lieutenant Colonel the rest of his life. So he took four lessons in navigation, got a crew of seaworthy friends, and prepared for the great test. His loving wife decided that if he was to drown, she wanted to drown with him. She took cooking lessons for weeks from her married daughter, so that Georgie would sign her on as ship's cook. She insisted on standing on a board, balanced on a round can, so that she would roll as she cooked. She always said later she could never have made it without that rigorous training, as she found that, like Nelson, she was always seasick at sea!

However, while she had never learned to cook, she had always made superb preserves — it was her family chore while she was growing up — and here are three of her favorites.

Avalon Grape Conserve

SIX JARS:

1 cup sugar
½ cup water
Cook to syrup.
3 cups white seedless grapes
3 tablespoons fresh chopped mint
Pinch of salt
A few drops of spearmint essence

Cook until the consistency of honey and place in sterilized jars.

Avalon Strawberry Jam

THREE PINTS:

1 quart strawberries
2 tablespoons lemon juice
Boil together 2 minutes.
Add 1 quart of sugar, boil together 5 minutes.

Remove from the fire and stir occasionally during about 24 hours. When the jam has thickened, put in sterilized jars.

Avalon Cranberry and Orange Relish

TWO PINTS:

1 pound of cranberries
Peel and juice of 1 orange

Put through the food grinder, add sugar to taste, and let stand 12 hours before serving. This is lovely with turkey.

Let's Go South
of the Border

THIS DELICIOUS and surprising "cocktail food" dish is from so far south of the border that it has to be explained. It comes from Panama. It is so easy to fix, and so delicious that everyone who has ever eaten it wants the recipe even after they find out that it is, oh! horrors, RAW FISH!

Seviche

FOR TEN OR TWELVE:

1 pound raw fillets of white, firm fish

or

of shrimp, that have been cooked for 10 minutes
Juice of 6 limes
3 onions, chopped fine
2 tomatoes, chopped fine
1 small, hot yellow pepper, chopped fine
(pickled hot peppers can be used)
1 green pepper, chopped fine
Garlic, parsley, salt, pepper and Tabasco

Mix well, cover and chill for at least 6 hours. Serve with crackers. The hot pepper and the lime actually cook the fish.

We must turn to Spain for this, but this Spanish cousin tastes perfectly wonderful when the weather is in the 90°'s and it's too hot to cook. Serve it in glass bowls, please.

Gazpacho

FOR FOUR OR FIVE:

Garlic
6 large ripe tomatoes, peeled, seeded and finely
  chopped
2 cucumbers, peeled, seeded and finely chopped
½ cup of red and green sweet peppers, minced
½ cup onion, minced
2 cups fresh tomato juice
⅛ cup olive oil
3 tablespoons lemon juice
Salt, pepper, Tabasco

Rub the bowls with a cut clove of garlic. Mix all ingredients together, and chill. Serve in individual, chilled bowls; add an ice cube to each bowl and sprinkle with chopped parsley and mint. A glob of sour cream is good, too.

One of the good things contributed by the "bad old days" is a taste for Mexican-Spanish cooking. There have been some fabulous dinners served from Fort Lewis, Washington, to Fort Myer, Virginia, that were inspired by the land of the bean and the chili pepper. And always, when you think of these dishes, think of Ice Cold Beer beside them. Here is a perfect dish for Sunday brunch, or an easy lunch, or supper after a football game.

Huevos Rancheros I

FOR FOUR:

- 2 tablespoons olive oil
- 2 tablespoons butter
- 1 large ripe tomato, chopped fine
- 1 or 2 hot peppers, chopped fine
- 1 large grated onion
- 1 green pepper, chopped fine
- Salt, garlic, vinegar
- 6 well-beaten eggs
- 2 tablespoons (or more to taste) chili powder

Heat oil and butter in a large covered skillet and cook all the vegetables slowly together till they form a thick sauce. Add seasonings, eggs, and scramble lightly. Chopped cervelat may be added.

Huevos Rancheros II

TWO EGGS APIECE:

Make the sauce as before, but don't beat your eggs, break them gently into the sauce and poach. The Spanish nickname for this is "Ox eyes" and they really do look at you in a knowing way.

There is nothing that takes the place of chili con carne in the American diet. Not even ham and eggs. However, there are chilies and chilies and anyone who has ever been stationed in the West will argue for hours about the difference. The following recipe is the best there is. It's so good that it can be made 2 gallons at a time and frozen. Never forget that chili, stew, and chowder all taste better after they have "sagashawaited" for 24 hours. Make this the day before the party. (This has a secret ingredient!)

REAL Chili con Carne

FOR SIX:

- 5 medium onions, chopped fine
- 2 garlic cloves, chopped fine
- 2 tablespoons of butter or olive oil
- 6 tablespoons chili powder (or more)
- 1 tablespoon flour
- 2 teaspoons ground coriander
- 2 teaspoons cumin seed
- 2 teaspoons orégano
- 2 #2 cans of tomatoes
- 2 cups water
- 4 tablespoons sugar
- 1 tablespoon salt
- 2 squares unsweetened chocolate (the secret is out!)

Fry onion and garlic in fat until it is golden brown and limp. Mix the chili powder, flour and all the herbs together and stir into the onions. Cook 3 minutes and then add the tomatoes and water. Cook to a simmer and season with sugar, salt and chocolate. Stir until dissolved and then cook an hour longer. The sauce should be about like gravy. It can be thinned with tomato juice.

This amount of sauce will take 4 pounds of beef, cut very fine — almost like hamburger, and will feed six people well. Cook the beef in the sauce until tender. To improve this dish, add two cans of chili beans. Please remember to let this stand overnight!

Every nation has its own way with chicken. Our Mexican cousins have one that is simple but subtle, and many years ago a visiting French General partook of this delicacy and said, with a sigh, "The aroma of my country, with the sultry promise of yours!" Please try this on the family and adjust the seasonings to suit.

Arroz con Pollo

FOR FOUR:

- 1 3-pound chicken
- 2 tablespoons olive oil
- 1 cup rice
- 1 onion, chopped
- 1 large, ripe tomato, chopped
- 1 green pepper, chopped
- 1 teaspoon orégano
- Salt, pepper and garlic

Dress, singe, and wash chicken. Separate at joints. Heat

oil in a deep kettle and fry the chicken to a golden brown. Add rice and stir over low heat until the rice has absorbed the oil and turned golden. Drop in vegetables and fry gently for 5 minutes. Add 3 cups boiling water, seasonings, cover tightly, and cook gently till the rice is fluffy.

Here is another!

Mexican Chicken Stew

FOR FIVE:

1 fowl, cut up
¼ cup olive oil
1 teaspoon salt
¼ teaspoon pepper
2 sliced onions
1 clove garlic, chopped
2 shredded green peppers
1½ tablespoons flour
¼ teaspoon ground cloves
½ teaspoon chili powder
2 cups canned tomatoes
¾ cup sherry
⅓ cup sliced stuffed olives

Brown the chicken in oil in a large pan and sprinkle with salt and pepper. Remove chicken and sauté onions, garlic and green pepper in the oil. Stir in flour, cloves, chili and tomato. Bring to a boil and cook 5 minutes. Add chicken, wine, cover and simmer till tender. Add olives just before serving.

And another!

Mexican Chicken with Orange Juice

FOR THREE OR FOUR:

1 cut-up fryer
3 tablespoons butter
12 blanched almonds
1 cup chopped pineapple
2 cups orange juice
Salt and pepper
½ cup seeded raisins
Dash of cloves and cinnamon
1 tablespoon flour mixed to a paste with 2 tablespoons
   cold water

Brown chicken in skillet, add all other ingredients except the flour paste. Cover the skillet and simmer for 45 minutes. Add flour paste, and cook until gravy is thickened, about 8 minutes. Garnish with avocado slices and serve sauce separately.

Here is another brunch favorite. There are as many variations of this as there are interesting things in your larder, but this basic idea is a good beginner.

Hot Tamale Pie

FOR FOUR:

- 1 cup yellow corn meal
- 3 cups boiling water
- 1 chopped onion
- ½ teaspoon chili powder (or more)
- 1 can tomato soup
- 2 tablespoons butter
- 1 pound hamburger
- 1 cup sliced, pitted ripe olives

Make a corn-meal mush with the corn meal and water. Line a casserole with the mush, leaving enough for a final topping on the dish. Mix the other ingredients, put them in the casserole, cover with the mush and cook in the oven for 30 minutes at 325°.

This time we go as far south of the border as one can get! This is also good for brunch or supper, and is a dandy way to use up leftover rice.

Arroz Argentina

FOR FOUR OR FIVE:

Mix:
- 2 cups cooked rice
- 3 tablespoons chopped green pepper
- ½ cup stewed raisins
- Tabasco, salt
- ¼ cup melted butter
- 1 small onion, chopped
- 2 tablespoons catsup
- Grated cheese

Place the mixture in a casserole, top with grated cheese, and bake 15 minutes at 400°.

Here is something else to do with the tough Mexican beef — could it be that bullfighting had something to do with it? Anyhow, this turns the fiercest bull into the gentlest calf.

Mexican Beef with Orange

FOR SIX:

2 cloves garlic
½ teaspoon ground cloves
Freshly ground pepper
1 teaspoon coriander
¾ teaspoon salt

Pound these into a paste.

Make cuts in a 3 lb. piece of round steak and force some paste into each cut. Put meat into a heavy skillet with ½ cup water, 1 bay leaf, one onion and a little salt, and simmer till tender. Cool, cut into thin slices and cover with orange juice. Let steak marinate overnight in icebox, turning occasionally. Garnish with orange slices, serve cold.

This one doesn't quite make the border, as it is from California, but it traveled in Mexico for some time, right after the War Between the States, in the brain of Colonel George Hugh Smith, C.S.A. He was widely traveled, and a lover of good food, and California in those days was a long way away from anywhere and he couldn't get East Indian chutney to go with his cold roast beef, which he loved. So, he invented:

California Chutney

ONE QUART:

9 stewed prunes
1 large apple
1 large onion
½ cup seedless raisins
½ cup canned tomatoes
¾ cup vinegar
¼ teaspoon salt
1 cup brown sugar
½ teaspoon dry mustard
Dash of cinnamon, mace and cayenne pepper

Put fruit and onion through the grinder, add to the remaining ingredients and simmer 20 minutes. Serve cold.

Chili con Carne, or Mexican Chicken both require a salad. There is always Guacamole, and very good it is too, but oh, try this!

Fire and Ice Tomatoes

FOR SIX OR EIGHT:

Skin and quarter 6 large, ripe, firm tomatoes. Slice one large green pepper into strips, and slice one large red onion into rings. Place in a bowl and cover with the following sauce:

Mix:
  ¾ cup vinegar
  4½ teaspoons sugar
  ¼ cup cold water
  1½ teaspoons celery salt
  ½ teaspoon salt
  Cayenne pepper and black pepper

Bring to a boil and boil furiously for 1 minute. While still hot, pour over the vegetables. Chill, covered. Just before serving, add one sliced cucumber.

The good thing about this is that you can use the "juice" over and over again. Sometimes I add the juice from a jar of dill pickles, just for a change.

Guacamole
(In case you didn't know what it was)

ONE HALF AVOCADO APIECE:

Very ripe avocadoes
Grated onion
Salt and pepper
Juice from hot pickled peppers
Dash of chili powder
Dash of Tabasco

Mix puréed avocado with the other ingredients until it is soft but of the consistency of mashed potatoes. Chill.

Important: If you leave the avocado seeds lying on top of the mixture until serving, it will not turn black.

Mexican Onion and Orange Salad

FOR FOUR OR FIVE:

Peel 2 oranges and slice into paper-thin circles. Slice one red onion paper thin. Add sliced, pitted ripe olives, and chill in a marinade of tart French dressing. Serve on lettuce leaves.

This dessert is Spanish in origin, but graces many a meal of Mexican type and is a lifesaver when company comes at the last minute.

Mexican Flan

ONE EGG APIECE:

Eggs
Sugar
Cocoa
Sherry
Cinnamon

Separate the eggs. To the yolks, add ½ teaspoon sugar, ½ teaspoon cocoa, 1 teaspoon of sherry per yolk, beat well and chill. Beat the whites until stiff and fold into the yolk mixture just before serving. Serve in individual glasses, and sprinkle each serving with a dash of cinnamon.

This next dessert is a wanderer without a home, but it is the perfect finish to a red-hot Mexican meal.

Lemon Granita

FOR SIX:

Boil 2 cups of sugar and 4 cups of water for 5 minutes. Add the grated rind of one lemon and from ½ to 1 cup of lemon juice. Cool and freeze, without stirring, until it forms a granular mass — 4 or 5 hours. Spoon into individual glasses and, over each serving pour 2 tablespoons of Crème de menthe.

Let's Take the Curse
off Vegetables

THERE ARE peas that make us happy, there are peas that make us blue, but the peas that make the world all sunshine, are these peas that I bring to you.

French Peas

FOR FOUR:

2 pounds shelled peas
1 can chicken broth
1 head lettuce, shredded
1 teaspoon sugar
Salt, pepper, nutmeg, butter

Cook the peas in the broth, add the lettuce and seasonings for the last 5 minutes. Drain, butter, and serve.

New England does not have the last word on baked beans. This is a very tasty recipe, and strangely enough, it is good cold.

Brown Beans from Izmir

FOR FOUR OR FIVE:

1 pound brown beans
1 onion, chopped
1 carrot, chopped
½ cup olive oil
1 tomato, chopped
Salt and cayenne

Wash the beans, soak overnight, boil till soft, and drain, saving the stock. Brown onions and carrot in the oil, add tomato and seasoning and cook 5 minutes. Pour in 1 cup bean stock, add the beans, and cook slowly 20 minutes.

This is a curious discovery, but oddly satisfying. Men seem to like it a lot and it's good with steak, or hamburgers, or cold roast beef.

Steermate

ONE TOMATO AND HALF AN ONION APIECE:

Sauté thick onion slices in butter until golden brown, push them to one side of the skillet, and sauté thick tomato slices until golden brown on both sides. Stir in

¾ cup of sour cream and let it brown slowly. Sprinkle with sweet basil.

Rice is always nice but this is a little bit nicer.

Orange Rice

FOR FOUR OR FIVE:

⅔ cup finely diced celery, with leaves included
1 medium onion, finely diced
¼ cup butter
1 cup orange juice, fresh, frozen or canned
Enough water to make up the liquid to cook the rice
    by directions on package.
1 teaspoon salt
Dash of dried thyme
2 tablespoons grated orange rind
1 cup rice

Cook celery and onion in butter till tender. Add liquid, salt and thyme and rind. Bring to a boil and add rice. Cook covered over low heat till tender.

This is delicious with chicken or duck.

These carrots are fine at a dinner party and men love them.

Carrots in Cognac

FOR FIVE OR SIX:

Scrape three dozen tender young carrots. Melt 1 cup butter in a baking dish, add carrots, a dash of salt, and a teaspoonful of sugar. Sprinkle with ⅛ cup cognac.

Cover baking dish and bake in a moderate oven for 1 hour or less, until carrots are tender but not brown.

This is good as a luncheon dish, and superb with veal of any kind.

Tomato Pudding

FOR FIVE:

2 6-ounce cans of tomato paste
6 tablespoons brown sugar
Salt
¼ cup water
1 cup fresh bread crumbs, without crusts
¼ cup melted butter
Dash of dried basil

Heat tomato paste to boiling point, add sugar and a dash of salt. Rinse cans with the water, add bread crumbs. Put the bread crumbs in a covered casserole, pour the melted butter over them, add the tomato paste, basil, and cover. Bake 30 minutes at 375°. Keep covered till served, otherwise it will "fall."

Spinach can be as good as Popeye pretends it is.

Swedish Spinach

FOR THREE OR FOUR:

1½ pounds spinach, or 1 package chopped frozen spinach
3 tablespoons flour
Salt and pepper
2 tablespoons butter
¾ cup cream

Cook spinach till tender, chop, drain and allow to cool. Add flour, salt and pepper, stirring slowly. Heat butter, add cream, add spinach slowly, stirring constantly. Cook for about 5 minutes.

This is real "party food" and certainly takes the place of potatoes.

Perfect Corn Pudding

FOR SIX:

2½ cups of corn (about 7 ears)
2 tablespoons flour
1 teaspoon salt
¼ teaspoon pepper
1½ tablespoons butter, melted
2 eggs
1½ cups milk

Preheat oven to 325°. With the tip of a sharp knife,

cut kernels down through the middle of each row of corn, then with the blade of the knife, scrape down ears to press out all pulp, into a large bowl. Sprinkle the flour, salt and pepper over the corn, add the butter and mix well. Break the eggs into a small bowl, beat lightly with a fork, add milk, blend well, and stir into the corn mixture. Pour it all into a greased baking dish, bake in the center of the oven. The pudding is done when a knife stuck into the center comes out clean. (About 70 minutes.) Serves 6.

There is nothing common about the common cabbage when it is cooked this way.

Cabbage and Celery Casserole

FOR FIVE:

½ cup chopped celery
5 tablespoons butter
3½ cups chopped cabbage (1 small head)
1 cup white sauce
1 tablespoon of chopped pimento, or green pepper or both
Salt, pepper, dash of dry mustard
½ cup dry bread crumbs

Cook the celery in 3 tablespoons of butter for 10 minutes. Add the cabbage and cook 10 minutes longer, over low heat. Pour into a buttered casserole, add white sauce and chopped peppers. Season. Cover with bread crumbs, dot with butter and bake at 350° for 20 minutes.

Instead of potatoes and rice, try something nice.

Glazed Bananas

ONE BANANA APIECE:

6 large, firm ripe bananas
3 tablespoons lemon juice
1 cup sugar
4 tablespoons butter

Peel and scrape the bananas, roll them in the lemon juice and then in the sugar. Sauté in butter, basting till the fruit is golden brown all over.

(If you want to turn these into dessert, add some dark rum to the butter!)

Banana Boats

ONE BANANA APIECE:

Take as many bananas as you need, slit the skin down the curved side, and slide your finger along each side of the fruit to loosen the skin; put a slip of butter on each side of the fruit and bake at 350° till the skins are black.

Let's Have a Drink

THERE were MEN in those days!

Horse Gunner's Punch

FOR TWELVE TO FIFTEEN:

- 1 fifth rye whiskey
- 4 cups strong black tea
- ½ pint gin
- 2 ounces Benedictine
- 1 cup lemon juice
- 1 fifth claret

1 pint Jamaica rum
½ pint cognac
2 cups orange juice

Let the mixture stand for 2 hours or more, to blend.
Sweeten to taste and pour over a block of ice.

This is the prince of punches, but don't underestimate
it! It's as powerful as it is delicious. It can be kept bottled too, if there is any left over, and gains in power as
it ages. I knew a Lieutenant Colonel at Fort Smith, Ar-
kansas, who was planning to have his whole battalion in
on New Year's Day, and when he came to make the
punch, lo, the only receptacle in the house that was big
enough was the diaper pail! It was the best bunch of
punch he ever made! Later, that evening, while they

PLEASE NOTE:		
1 jigger	equals	3 tablespoons
1 pony		2 tablespoons
1 dash		⅓ teaspoon
1 split		1 cup
1 liqueur glass		2 tablespoons
1 sherry glass		2 ounces
1 cocktail glass		4 or 5 ounces
1 rickey glass		8 ounces
1 highball glass		1¾ cups
1 wineglass		4 ounces
1 champagne glass		4 ounces
1 old-fashioned glass		8 ounces

were walking it off around the reservoir, they met a talking duck. The fact that the duck turned out to really *be*
a duck, and that it had been in vaudeville for fifteen
years, did nothing to make them feel better next morn-
ing. This is a three-day operation. You MUST make it
the day before, and you MUST beware the day after!

Philadelphia Fish House Punch

FOR FIFTEEN:

- 1 quart water
- 8 teaspoons *green* tea
- 1 pint lemon juice, with peels
- 1 pint grape juice
- 1 pint orange juice
- ¼ pound sugar
- 2 quarts bourbon whiskey
- 1 quart brandy
- 1 quart dark rum
- 1 pint peach brandy

Bring the water to a boil, add tea, fruit juices, lemon
peels and sugar. Steep 10 minutes, strain, cool, and add
to liquor. Let stand 24 hours before using. This should
take care of fifteen people very well indeed.

Claret Punch

FOR TEN TO TWELVE:

This is a most refreshing drink, and can be kept bottled
in the icebox for summer afternoons, without the carbonated water, of course. Cucumber sandwiches with
this, and the day is made.

Dissolve 3 tablespoons of sugar in the juice of 3 lemons; add 2 jiggers of Cointreau, 2 jiggers of cognac. Add

1 quart chilled claret, 1 quart of chilled sauterne and 1 quart chilled carbonated water. Pour over a block of ice.

Claret Lemonade

TWO JIGGERS OF CLARET PER GLASS:

Per glass, 1 teaspoon of fine sugar, the juice of 1 lemon, 2 jiggers claret. Fill the glass with ice cubes and carbonated water.

These three punches are perfect for weddings, garden parties, or life in a warm climate. California champagne is fine for these.

Moselle Cup

FOR TWELVE TO FIFTEEN:

Peel and slice 6 oranges thin, put the slices in a bowl and sprinkle with 1 cup fine sugar. Cover with 1 bottle Moselle wine. Cover the bowl and let the fruit marinate for an hour. Add 1 bottle chilled Moselle, 3 bottles of chilled champagne, and a block of ice.

Rhine Wine Cooler

FOR FIFTEEN TO TWENTY:

Pour over ice 1 cup Falernum, the juice of 18 limes, 3 cups dry sherry, 2 cups cognac, 2 cups strong tea, 6 bottles of Rhine wine. Garnish with slices of cucumber. (Yes, it brings out the flavor of the punch!)

Rhenish Punch

FOR TWELVE:

Combine in a pitcher ¼ cup of peach liqueur, ¼ cup Benedictine, 2 oranges and 2 lemons, both sliced thin, and a bunch of mint. Allow to stand for 2 hours. Pour over ice in a punch bowl, add 1 cup of washed and hulled strawberries, and 2 bottles of cold Rhine wine.

This is the prettiest thing you ever saw!

Here are two exotic punches, from our friends over the water. Punch has acquired a bad name in many places because some people make it with inferior wines, and make it too sweet. Properly made, it is delicious, stimulates conversation, and leaves no hangover.

Empire Punch

Put 3 or 4 ice cubes in a tall glass. Pour over 1 teaspoon each of Benedictine, cognac, Cointreau, and 2 jiggers of claret. Blend gently, fill with champagne, and garnish with mint.

Montego Bay Punch

FOR TWELVE TO FIFTEEN:

Pour into a bowl 1 bottle Jamaica rum, 1 bottle light rum, 1 cup apricot liqueur, 2 cups orange juice; add 2 oranges and 2 lemons, unpeeled but sliced thin. Set this bowl in cracked ice, and at serving time add 2 quarts of chilled ginger beer. (Ginger ale will do, but it's a little sweet.)

Now, let's switch from co-o-o-o-ol to HOT!

Hot Spiced Whiskey

In a china mug combine ¼ teaspoon powdered cloves, ¼ teaspoon grated nutmeg, 1 stick cinnamon, 1 teaspoon sugar. Heat gently 2½ ounces of bourbon and pour over the spices. Let steep 10 minutes, then fill the mug with boiling water.

Better Hot Buttered Rum

Put into a silver or pewter mug a strip of orange peel, 2 teaspoons brown sugar, ½ jigger of warm golden rum. Set fire to the rum and let it burn out. Add another jigger of golden rum, 1 teaspoon butter, part of a cinnamon stick, and ¼ teaspoon each of ground cloves and ground allspice. Fill the mug with boiling *cider* and stir.

Both of these drinks sound as if they came from a detective story, but it must have been a very good yarn.

Singapore Gin Sling

In a cocktail shaker half full of ice, combine 1 teaspoon bar syrup, juice of ½ lime, 1 jigger kirsch, 1½ jiggers gin, a dash of Angostura bitters. Shake and strain into a highball glass, fill with ice and soda.

Bar Syrup
(In case you don't know)

Boil together for 5 minutes 3 cups sugar, 1 cup water, bottle and save.

Maharajah's Burra Peg

Put 3 or 4 ice cubes in a highball glass, pour in 1 jigger cognac. Fill the glass with chilled champagne, and garnish with lemon peel.

With those paragons of hospitality — General and Mrs. "Snake" Young of the Engineers — Hats Off!!

Dow Punch

FOR TWELVE TO FIFTEEN:

This is an old family recipe, which is really a variant of Fish House Punch, but somewhat lighter and equally insinuating. Quantities are given in ounces and should be measured accurately in a graduated measuring glass. Mix several days in advance, and let stand in corked containers in a cool place (but *not* in the icebox). To serve, pour over a large piece of ice in a punch bowl. The amount given below will serve a dozen people more or less.

Dark rum (best quality)	15 ounces
Light rum (Barcardi Gold Seal preferred)	11 ounces
Cognac (good quality of Courvoisier preferred)	11 ounces
Peach brandy	5 ounces
French sauterne (any reasonably good brand)	40 ounces
Lemon juice	13 ounces
Total	95 ounces

And here — the General allows 5 ounces of hard liquor per evening for "serious drinking." The wine can be scaled down accordingly.

With this drink, let's have —

These can be made ahead of time in any amount and kept in the icebox.

Cheese Wafers

MAKES THREE DOZEN:

1 full cup finely grated yellow cheese
2 cups sifted flour
Salt and cayenne pepper
½ pound melted butter

Knead on a board until well blended, form into rolls about 1 inch in diameter, wrap in wax paper and chill. Cut into rounds and bake at 325° for 10 minutes. (Warning: Let them cool a little before eating — they are divinely crumbly.)

Hot Olive Puffs

FOR TWO DOZEN:
1 cup grated sharp cheese
3 tablespoons soft butter
½ cup sifted flour
Salt, pepper and cayenne.
24 stuffed olives

Mix the cheese, butter, flour and seasonings well; wrap about 1 teaspoon of the resulting dough around each olive, and chill. Bake at 400° 10 to 15 minutes. Serve hot.

And with this drink, let's have —

These look so pretty with the golden cheese-things.

Stuffed Pickle Slices

SIX SLICES TO A PICKLE:

Core large dill pickles and stuff with the following:

(1) Roquefort and cream cheese, blended
(2) Crabmeat and Russian Dressing
(3) Chopped tongue and mayonnaise

Chill and slice into round ½ inch thick

New Orleans Shrimp Bowl

FOR ABOUT TWENTY:

⅛ cup olive oil
2 tablespoons chili sauce
1 tablespoon prepared horseradish
½ teaspoon paprika
3 tablespoons chopped onion
3 tablespoons lemon juice
2 tablespoons catsup
1 tablespoon prepared mustard
Cayenne pepper
1½ pounds cooked cleaned shrimp

Marinate together about 3 hours, and serve with toothpicks around the bowl.

Let's Travel – East
of Gibraltar

THE FIRST TIME I tasted this was in a restaurant in Washington, D.C. But to taste it on a schooner, anchored off the island of Lemnos, with the fragrance of the lemon orchard washing over the dinner table, doesn't make it any better — just more habit-forming.

Greek Lemon Soup

FOR SIX TO EIGHT:

⅓ cup rice
6 cups chicken stock
4 egg yolks
Grated rind and juice of 2 lemons
1 cup sour cream
Salt, cayenne pepper
1 cup light cream
1 cup whipped cream
Paprika

Wash the rice in a little water to remove all excess starch, and drain thoroughly. Add rice slowly to boiling chicken stock and cook for 30 minutes, till the rice is very soft. Rub through a fine strainer. Beat the egg yolks thoroughly with the grated rind of 1 lemon. Slowly add the juice of 2 lemons. Mix in the sour cream and slowly pour on the hot soup, making sure the liquid does not curdle. Season, and stir over a slow fire till the soup coats the back of a wooden spoon. Chill thoroughly. Stir in the light cream. Serve in individual bowls, surrounded by crushed ice. Put a tablespoon of whipped cream on top of each and garnish with remaining lemon rind and a little paprika.

The fun of traveling is often enhanced by the food (and the wine) of the country. Photographs fade, but recipes get better and better as they are used more and more, and the smell of onions in olive oil will always conjure up Italy: add a little dill weed, and see the crowded bazaars of Turkey: lemons scent the air and food of Greece; thyme blends them all.

Roman Luncheon Eggs

ONE EGG APIECE:

Scramble eggs in butter quite firm. Place each portion in a flat soup plate and pour hot consommé over it. Sprinkle generously with Parmesan cheese.

La Piperade

FOR FOUR:

1 onion, chopped
1 green pepper, sliced thin
3 tablespoons olive oil
1 tomato, peeled and seeded
Garlic, salt, pepper
6 eggs
Ham slices

Sauté onion and pepper in olive oil. When limp, add tomato and seasonings. Simmer, covered, until it reaches the purée stage. Add the eggs and stir only enough to mix lightly with the purée. Cook slowly until eggs are set. Serve on thin slices of warm ham.

Here are two Yugoslavs who have deserted to the west — they deserve attention and kind treatment.

Fried Cheese

ABOUT FOUR CHUNKS PER PERSON:

Cut cheddar cheese into chunks 1 by ½ by 3 inches. Dip
them into beaten egg, then into cracker crumbs, then into
the eggs again, then into the crumbs again, and fry in
deep fat till golden brown and serve hot.

Twabchichi

ALLOW ½ POUND OF BEEF PER PERSON:

Chop ground round beef very fine and make into little
rolls the size of your finger. Broil these lightly, they
should be very rare, and serve simply smothered under
chopped fried onions and chopped fried green peppers.

There is no lamb in the world like the lamb in Turkey.
They graze on banks of thyme. The Turks butcher the
lambs so young that it takes the whole back end of one
lamb to feed a family of five. The lambs are brought up
with the Turkish family, petted and fattened outside the
door, and killed and eaten with loving appreciation. First
of all, of course —

Shish Kebab

FOR FOUR:

2 pounds lamb, cut into 1-inch cubes
Juice of 1 lemon
1 tablespoon olive oil
Salt and pepper
1 medium tomato, sliced
Green pepper, or eggplant, or mushrooms
Bay leaves

Rub the meat with the lemon juice and oil, put in a deep dish, sprinkle with salt and pepper, cover with tomatoes and onion and a few bay leaves. Chill for at least 6 hours. Arrange the meat on spits with an occasional bay leaf, alternating meat with onion, tomato, a slice of green pepper, or a chunk of eggplant, or a mushroom. Broil and serve.

Gardener's Kebab
(Lamb stew supreme)

FOR SIX:

- 2 pounds lamb, cut into ½-inch cubes
- 6 tablespoons butter
- 4 carrots, ¼-inch slices
- 2 medium tomatoes
- 25 tiny onions
- Salt
- 1 cup shelled green peas
- 1 red pepper, chopped
- 1 teaspoon fresh dill weed (or dried)

Cook the meat in butter till the color changes. Add carrots, cover tightly, and cook over very low heat for an hour. Add tomatoes, onions, salt, peas and pepper. Cover and cook for ½ hour. Only if necessary, add a little bouillon. When the meat is tender, stir in the dill and serve.

Turlu
(This is even better!)

FOR SIX:

2 medium onions, sliced
¼ cup butter
¾ pound lamb, diced
¾ pound string beans
3 medium tomatoes
2 large zucchini
2 medium eggplants
4 large green peppers
¼ pound okra
Salt and pepper

Fry onions in butter till golden brown. Add meat, ½ cup water, and simmer till tender. Prepare the vegetables by stringing the beans, peeling and slicing the tomatoes, cutting the zucchini and eggplant into 2-inch cubes, dicing the peppers. When meat is nearly tender, add 1 cup water, and then, in this order, beans, zucchini, eggplant, okra, tomatoes and peppers. Season. Cover tightly and cook ½ hour.

The Circassian women were supposed to be the most beautiful in the Near-Eastern world, and every sultan wanted Circassian concubines, with their golden hair and blue eyes, and their proud, wild ways. However, there must have been something more to them than just looks, because they left us this delicate memory.

Circassian Chicken

FOR SIX TO TEN (A LARGE TURKEY WILL SERVE TEN):

Boil a chicken (or a turkey) in a medium amount of water, seasoning it with bay leaf, salt, pepper and onion. Per person, provide one handful of shelled walnuts and two slices of stale, whole-wheat bread without crusts. Break the cooked fowl into fairly small pieces, and place in a deep platter. Skim the fat from the broth. Grind the nuts, gizzard, heart, liver, skin and bits of meat from the neck and legs, putting it twice through the fine grinder. Soak the bread in the warm broth. Mix the bread and the ground nuts and meat and add enough broth until it is just runny. Place it on top of the cooked meat, and sprinkle with paprika. Chill.

This is a most heavenly buffet dish, summer or winter.

The people of the Near East are very fond of stuffing things — they stuff peppers and grape leaves and eggplant, and call the stuffed object a "dolma." They also call a fountain pen a "stuffed pencil." The following dish is delicious on a buffet, and a delicious way to serve zucchini.

Stuffed Zucchini

FOR SIX:

Peel 3 pounds of zucchini, cut them into 3-inch slices, and remove the center pulp to make a hollow tube. Combine the pulp with ½ pound of ground lamb, 2 large chopped onions, 1 chopped tomato and ½ bunch of chopped parsley. Add ½ cup uncooked rice, 1 teaspoon salt, and a ¼ teaspoon each of black pepper and chopped dried mint; blend well. Stuff the zucchini tubes and arrange them side by side in an oven-proof pan; cover with ½ cup of tomato purée. Add 2 cups of water and a couple of bouillon cubes and bring the water to boil on top of the stove. Then bake the dish in a moderate oven, 350° for 50 minutes.

The people of the Near East love cold vegetables cooked with oil. These sound disgusting, but are simply delicious. Here are two salads that will prove it —

Artichokes Byzantine

FOR SIX:

6 large artichokes
Juice of 2 lemons
2 medium onions, sliced
1 tablespoon sugar
⅔ cup olive oil
Salt and pepper
1 cup water

Cut the tops off the artichokes and place the bottoms in a large covered pot. Add in this order: lemon juice, sliced onions, sugar, oil, seasoning and water. Cover tightly and cook over a medium fire for 1 hour without removing the cover. Serve cold or hot.

Beans the Teeth Love

FOR SIX:

2 pounds long green beans
Salt
Juice of ½ lemon
1 large onion, quartered
1 large tomato, quartered
½ cup olive oil
2 cups water
1 tablespoon sugar
Pepper
Sage and mint (a pinch of each)
Lettuce
Hard-boiled egg
Olives

Wash, trim and break the beans in half. Toss them in salt and lemon juice. Stack like a woodpile in the bottom of a covered pot, leaving a well into which you put the onion and tomato. Pour in olive oil and water. Add sugar and seasonings. Cover and cook slowly for 2 hours, or until water is gone. When cooked, let cool in pot. Put a plate over the top of the pot and reverse onto plate. Serve on lettuce, garnish with hard-boiled egg sections and olives.

This Italian dish has a secret ingredient. If you don't tell your family, they will never guess what it is.

Foie de Veau Italienne
(I put the title in French to keep the Secret)

FOR FIVE:

1 pound calves' liver (secret ingredient) sliced very
    thin
¼ cup butter
2 slices ham, minced
2 tablespoons onion, minced
3 tablespoons chopped parsley
¼ teaspoon sage
1 tablespoon flour
¾ cup sherry

Coat the liver slices with seasoned flour and sauté in
butter till golden brown on both sides. Remove to a
warm platter. Add the ham, onion, parsley and sage to
the hot butter and sauté until the onion is tender but
not brown. Stir the flour into a paste in the sherry; add,
season to taste, and simmer until thickened. Add the
liver and simmer just long enough to heat through.

The people of the Near East love desserts, but most
of them are far too sweet for most of us. They have en-
chanting names, though, such as "Ladies' Dimples" and
"Ladies' Thighs." However, here are three that melt in
the mouth, but leave the teeth intact.

Arabian Nights Baked Apples

FOR SIX:

Core 6 big, tart apples; peel a quarter way down from
the stem end, put in a covered pan, not quite touching;

fill the cavities with sugar, dust the tops with sugar, put in the peel of 2 oranges, red coloring, and ¾ cup of hot water. Cook slowly until tender.

Stuffing

Chop finely equal amounts of dates and figs, seasoned with cloves, cinnamon, and dark rum.

Put apples in a greased baking dish, stuff them, dust them with spices, pour the syrup they cooked in over them, and bake at 375° until they are done.

Honey Mousse

FOR SIX:

Beat the yolks of 6 fresh eggs together with 1½ cups of dark, strained honey. Stir over hot water until thickened. Chill and fold in the stiffly beaten whites of three eggs and 1 pint of whipped cream. Mold and freeze, without stirring.

Rose Petal Preserve

ABOUT ONE QUART:

1 pound or 1 quart of rose petals
1 quart water
3 to 6 pounds sugar
1 tablespoon lemon juice

Soak the rose petals in the water, covered with a damp cloth, until they have lost a good bit of color — about half an hour. Strain off the water and keep it in a covered jar. In a large agate or enamel kettle, make layers of sugar and petals. Pour on ⅛ of the rose water, press down, cover, and let stand 24 hours. Pour in the next third of the water and heat slowly. As the petals cook down, add the rest of the water, a little at a time. Continue to cook until thickened like conserve. Stir in the lemon juice and remove from the heat. Cool and store in 8 8-ounce paraffin-covered glasses.

Smells as good as it tastes!

Let's Have a Party

FOR A BRIDGE LUNCHEON in the cold weather, or for an after-the-game warm-up dish, the following is filling and delicious and subtly flavored.

My Lady's Soup

FOR SIX:

1 can cream of pea soup
1 can milk
Sherry to taste
1 can cream of mushroom soup
1 can crabmeat, canned or fresh

Heat them all together, over hot water. Sprinkle a little nutmeg on top.

And also, for the ladies!

Cold Cheese Soufflé

FOR SIX TO EIGHT:

1 envelope gelatin
¼ cup cold water
½ cup hot milk
1 teaspoon lemon juice
1 teaspoon onion juice
Salt, curry powder, dry mustard, Tabasco
2 cups grated Parmesan cheese
2 cups whipped cream

Soften the gelatin in the cold water, and dissolve it in the hot milk. Add juices and seasonings and stir well. Add cheese and blend. Fold in the whipped cream. Pour the mixture into a chilled mold that has been rinsed with cold water, and chill for 3 hours or until firmly set.

For a summer party, the following dish is almost too

pretty to eat, but as it must be made the day before, it is too good to resist.

Chaud-Froid of Chicken

FOR SIX:

1 canned whole chicken
1 grated onion
1 can condensed consommé
1 6-ounce can of mushrooms, drained
A pinch of dried rosemary and dried summer savory
6 small carrots
12 stuffed green olives

Very carefully, over hot water, melt the gravy from the chicken and save. Skin and bone the meat carefully, in order to make nice-looking pieces of meat. To the melted chicken gravy add onion and consommé. Bring to a boil and simmer for 20 minutes. Strain this, and add to it the mushrooms, and the herbs. Allow to cool. Wash and slice the carrots and simmer them in a very little water for 15 minutes. Drain, and cool. Pour the cooled broth into an oven-proof mold. Lay the chicken pieces, carrots, and olives in the broth to make a pretty effect when unmolded. Bake 30 minutes at 350°. Cool, then chill. After an hour, skim the fat from the dish. Chill overnight. Unmold when ready to serve and garnish with lettuce, cucumber strips, watercress, radishes. Serve with mayonnaise to which you have blended a little anchovy paste.

Cold ham, cold beef and cold turkey are always delicious at a party, with the infinite variety of salads that modern refrigeration make possible, but in the wintertime it's nice to have one hot dish. General and Mrs.

George S. Patton, Jr., always served one of the two following dishes at the parties they had between September and April. The beauty of these two is that you can use canned or frozen oysters.

Oyster Pie

FOR SIX:

1 pint oysters
1 hard-boiled egg, mashed
2 tablespoons chopped celery
Cracker crumbs, salt, A-1 Sauce, butter
Pie crust

Strain the oysters and lay them on a towel, saving the oyster liquor. Add all other ingredients to the liquor, bring to the boiling point and boil 3 minutes. Put the oysters in a buttered pie plate and pour the boiling liquid over them. Cover with pie crust, press down edges, prick the center and bake for ½ hour at 375°.

Avalon Scalloped Oysters

ALLOW ONE CUP OF OYSTERS APIECE.
A LARGE PYREX DISH WILL SERVE EIGHT
TO TEN:

Arrange crushed crackers and oysters in layers in a shallow baking dish. The top and bottom layers should be of crumbs, with no more than three layers of oysters. Season with pepper and dot with butter. Add cream until it just shows around the edges of the top layer. Let the dish stand for an hour before baking, and add more cream if it seems to have disappeared. Bake at 325° for 1½ hours.

In the 1900's, when all seemed well with the world, young men from the Ivy League colleges would frequently make a World Tour before settling down to cutting coupons and attending class reunions. The following recipe, until now, has been a family secret. This is a secret that's too good to keep. Don't forget — this must be made the day before to get the full flavor.

F. A.'s Indian Curry

1 large frying chicken
2½ cups milk
½ cup grated coconut
6 strips bacon
1 large grated onion
2 inches of fresh or candied ginger root
Dash of garlic
4 to 6 tablespoons curry powder
Milk from a fresh coconut, if possible
1 tablespoon flour
Salt, pepper, cayenne, a few drops of almond extract

Cook chicken in a quart of water. Cool, remove from bones and dice meat. Save the broth, put the bones back into the broth and cook it down to one-half volume. Scald the milk, add the coconut, and let it sit for 2 hours. Cook the bacon, remove from pan, and save. Sauté the onion in the fat until it is golden. Add ginger, garlic, curry powder and cook gently for about 3 minutes. Then add the milk and coconut (and the coconut milk, if you have it). Make a paste of flour and water and add to other ingredients, and stir until thickened. Then season to taste with the other seasonings. Let this simmer very gently for about 20 minutes. The sauce should then be strained, but if you have a blender, put the sauce in the blender and then strain it — this makes it richer. Add the chicken, and if necessary, thin with the chicken broth. Let sit overnight. Warm before serving and serve with boiled rice.

With the curry and rice, at least six of the following should be served in little dishes, to pile onto the curry:

Chopped crisp bacon	Grated coconut
Chopped peanuts	Chopped green onions
Raisins	Chopped anchovies
Chopped olives	"Bombay Duck" — a dried
Cubes of glazed bananas	fish from "speciality gro-
Chopped hard-boiled eggs	ceries"

You MUST serve mango chutney, to top it all. With this dinner goes a plain green salad, with French dressing, a centerpiece of ripe fruit, and coffee. P.S. — 3 cups of diced, cooked lamb is good, too.

Back in 1940 this whole party was "invented" by an army wife who had no maid. It has served her and her friends well for twenty years, mostly because it can ALL be done the day before!

REPT's Shrimp Dinner

FOR TWELVE TO FOURTEEN:

The following amount of sauce will take 7 pounds of shrimp and feed 12 to 14 people.

6 slices bacon
2 large grated onions
1 cup celery, diced
6 to 8 tablespoons olive oil
2 tablespoons flour

2 green peppers, chopped
2 #2 cans tomatoes
2 tablespoons vinegar
2 tablespoons sugar
4 (or more) tablespoons chili powder
1 clove garlic, crushed
Cayenne pepper to taste
½ teaspoon thyme
2 bay leaves
½ cup chopped parsley
1 tablespoon Worcestershire sauce
1 tablespoon horseradish
2 tablespoons lemon juice
1 teaspoon dry mustard
Paprika to taste
A dash of Tabasco
1 box frozen okra, or equivalent
½ pound mushrooms, or 2 small cans

Cook the bacon until crisp and remove from pan. Brown onions and celery in the bacon fat, and add olive oil. Add flour, peppers, bacon, tomatoes and seasonings. Simmer gently until it is a purée. This can be done the day before, in fact, it is better if it sits overnight. Add the okra, mushrooms and cooked cleaned shrimp one half hour before serving. Simmer them gently. If the sauce is too thick, thin it with tomato juice. Serve with boiled rice.

With this goes garlic-buttered French bread and vegetable salad.

Vegetable Salad

The day before: Cook 2 boxes of frozen mixed vegetables with a tablespoon of dried salad herbs and let them marinate overnight in French dressing. Just before the party, mix in a little mayonnaise and turn them out onto a bed of lettuce. Surround the vegetables with raw bits of onion, radishes, celery, green pepper, carrot curls and cauliflower buds. Beside the salad have a bowl of mayonnaise that has been pepped up with prepared horseradish and mustard.

Serve a dry red wine.

Fruit Cup

The dessert — 1 box each of frozen strawberries, raspberries, cherries and peaches. Drain the juice and boil it down to half its volume, and cool. Add to the frozen fruit, chopped apples, pineapple, grapes, melon balls, lichee nuts (canned) and bits of candied ginger. Pour juice over fruit and let sit at least 6 hours. If it seems too dry, add white wine.

And with it, Sponge Cake.

Finally —

Café Royale

2 quarts STRONG coffee
1 pint vanilla ice cream
1 quart brandy

Serve cold, in a punchbowl, with the ice cream floating on top.

They will come back next time you ask them!

One of the nicest parties we ever went to was at the home of a British officer, with whom we were sharing a so-called "hardship station." The British were paid at the local rate, and had a hard time making both ends meet, but with their usual spirited pride, they entertained on their camp chairs, and on trunk lockers with a table-cloth of local manufacture, and rose above the situation entirely. First we had sherry — this is a point to re-member — DON'T serve hard liquor with a cheese fondue, or you won't sleep a wink for a week. Then we went to the table where the fondue was bubbling over an alcohol flame. We each had a plate of toast cubes and a fork, and we dipped into the fondue and washed it down with cold white Greek wine. Later there was ham, salad and fruit. The fondue was the main event. The officer's wife had been to Switzerland to visit her son, who was in school there, and had brought back the cheese in her raincoat pocket.

Jacqueline's Swiss Fondue

FOR FIVE:

- 1 clove garlic
- 1¾ cups dry white wine (if possible, Fendant or Neuf-chatel)
- ¾ pound natural (if possible) Gruyère cheese, grated
- 3 teaspoons cornstarch
- 3 teaspoons kirschwasser
- Freshly grated black pepper

Rub bottom and sides of heat-proof casserole or chafing dish with garlic. Add wine. Heat wine to boiling point but do not let it boil. Add cheese, stirring constantly with a *wooden* spoon. When cheese is creamy and barely simmering, add the cornstarch, which has been blended with the kirsch. Stir the mixture till it bubbles and add pepper to taste. Place the casserole over a low alcohol flame and keep it hot, but not simmering. If it becomes too thick, add white wine a little at a time.

There are times when we have time to have a small dinner party, not a crush. Everyone has their favorite accompaniments to roast lamb, so all we will provide this time is the best roast lamb in the world.

Leg of Lamb Cantonese

FOR SIX TO EIGHT:

Leg of Lamb
Chinese Soy Bean Sauce, 1 bottle, 3 ounces or more
Strained honey

Trim all the fat you can from the leg of lamb. Rub with pepper and smear with honey, lavishly, on all sides. Place in a roasting pan on a rack with ¾ of an inch of water on the bottom of the pan. Preheat oven to 450°. Cook the lamb, uncovered, at 450° for ½ hour, basting with half the bottle of sauce at the end of the first 15 minutes. Reduce the heat and start basting about every 15 minutes. On the second basting, use up the other half of the soy bean sauce. Cook ½ hour per pound and add 20 minutes for luck. Remove the lamb, add about 2 tablespoons cornstarch, mixed with enough water to make a paste, to the pan juices, and cook till thickened.

The hot oven cooks the honey right away and more or less seals the juices into the lamb. The lamb will be very dark and the pan juices will be black, but the flavor is pure gold and the meat will be juicy and just right.

There are times when the ever-present ham and turkey just don't seem fancy enough. Many Christmases ago a sister died and left two heartbroken children with an aunt. Their father was overseas and it just seemed that

SOMETHING had to be done to make a Dickens-y Christmas that would be different and not remind anyone of the wonderful Christmases now past. So —

Roast Suckling Pig

FOR AT LEAST TWELVE:

1 10–15 pound piglet
1 tablespoon salt
1 teaspoon pepper
¾ teaspoon powdered thyme
2 teaspoons dry mustard
Fruit-almond stuffing

Wash the pig thoroughly, and dry inside and out (do have the butcher clean it for you). Mix salt, pepper, thyme and mustard and rub it all over the inside of the pig. Fill with stuffing, lace closed. Place a raw potato the size of an apple in the pig's mouth, and cover its ears with cooking foil. Put a piece of heavy-duty foil in the bottom of an open roasting pan (a dishpan is the right size) 12 inches longer than the pig. Place pig diagonally on foil, with its back legs forward, and turn foil up loosely around pig. Set diagonally in a 350° oven and roast 18 minutes per pound; 15 minutes before the pig is done, brush a mixture of ½ prepared mustard and ½ water over the skin. Remove the pig to a hot platter, put an apple in its mouth, cranberries in its eyes, and a

wreath of parsley around its ears. Pour drippings into a saucepan and make gravy.

Fruit Almond Stuffing

    1 pound almonds, blanched and shredded
    1½ pounds cooked, pitted prunes
    10 large apples, peeled, cored, sliced
    ¼ pound butter

Chop together and season with cloves and cinnamon.

They sang the Boar's Head Carol, and had a Merry Christmas.

Those of us not on the "tender meat list" have our little problems and for once, the Russians have solved a problem instead of posing it. Try this, taking out your feelings on the Russians in using the mallet, and you will thank them for —

Beef Stroganoff

FOR FIVE OR SIX:

    2½ pounds of round steak
    ¼ pound butter
    2 tablespoons chopped onion
    ½ pound sliced mushroom caps
    ½ pint sour cream
    Salt and pepper

Trim off all the fat from the beef. POUND with a mallet until it is ¼ inch thick. Cut into matchsticks 3 inches long and ¼ inch wide. Melt the butter in a covered pan, add the onion, and stir in the beef. Cook quickly for 2

minutes, turning once. Put the meat on a warm platter.
Add the mushrooms, cook 3 minutes. Return the beef
to the pan and warm again. Slowly stir in the sour cream,
salt and pepper to taste, and leave in a 300° oven, covered, for about 45 minutes.

Buttered noodles are delicious with this.

One of the Grand Old Ladies of the late U.S. Cavalry
(hats off!) had so many children she didn't know what
to do, and on a Colonel's pay — in the day when the
men played polo, and rode to hounds, and had to have
Peel boots from England, it was hard to know how to
feed the family, let alone have a party. But she had
parties just the same, seasoned with hospitality, warmed
with love, and served with courtesy. She always served:

Country Captain

FOR SIX:

1 old hen, or 12 chicken legs
3 onions, chopped
1 crushed clove garlic
1 tablespoon parsley, chopped
1 green pepper, chopped
1 teaspoon curry powder
Salt, pepper, butter
1 teaspoon dried thyme
2 #2 cans tomatoes
1 cup blanched, slivered almonds
1 cup seedless raisins

Soak chicken in cold water, skin, and roll in seasoned
flour. Fry until golden brown, and put into a roaster
with the following sauce: Sauté onion, garlic, parsley,

green pepper and seasoning in 2 tablespoons butter for 15 minutes. Add 1 cup of water, tomatoes, and cook till smooth. Pour over chicken and cook at 300° for an hour. Add nuts and raisins for the last 20 minutes. Serve with boiled rice.

The Class of '35 had a covered-dish supper at Carlisle Barracks that was a lesson to us all. Many classmates hadn't seen each other for fifteen years and some of the wives had never met. Therefore we all put our best foot forward, and this foot was the furthest of all in front.

Barley Pilaf

FOR EIGHT:

2 onions, chopped
¼ pound butter
1 quart rich chicken stock
½ pound mushrooms, sliced
1¾ cups pearl barley

To make a meat-and-barley dish, boil an old hen till she is tender and use the stock, saving the meat to go into the pilaf in small pieces.

Cook the mushrooms gently in the butter for 5 minutes, lift them out of the pot and cook the onions until they wilt. Pour the barley into the pot and *stir constantly* until it turns a dark golden brown (that is the flavor secret). Add the mushrooms and pour in 1¾ cups stock. Cover tightly and bake for ½ hour, in the oven, at 350°. Add another 1¾ cups stock, taste for seasoning, and bake ½ hour more. Add stock if barley becomes dry. Cook 15 minutes more. If you are going to add the chicken, add it for the last fifteen minutes.

Wife and
Mother Savers

THIS CHAPTER is dedicated to the last-minute rush that happens to the best of us, whether it's bridge or babies. The clock marches on, and there is nothing to eat in the house!

Easy Cheese Sauce

    2 tablespoons flour
    2 tablespoons bacon fat, oil or butter
    1 cup milk, fresh or canned
    ½ to 1 whole small jar quick-spread cheese
    Salt, pepper, cayenne

Mix flour into the melted fat, slowly add milk and cook until it begins to thicken; add cheese, and salt, pepper, cayenne to taste; cook, stirring, till smooth.

This sauce is good too on —

Stuffed Green Peppers

ONE PEPPER APIECE:

Parboil peppers, remove tops and seeds, stuff with left-over rice, or hamburger, or any combination of chopped meat, nuts, raisins, and crumbs. Place in an oven-proof dish and bake from 10 to 20 minutes. It's best to put a little water in the dish. Serve hot, covered with Easy Cheese Sauce.

And this sauce is good on —

Stuffed Egg Casserole

ALLOW TWO EGGS APIECE, HARD-BOILED:

Cut eggs in half, remove the yolks and mix them with mayonnaise, mustard, canned deviled ham, and salt and pepper. Fill the cavities, stick the eggs together again, put them in a casserole, cover them with Easy Cheese Sauce and bake at 350° till the sauce is bubbling.

Also good on this version of —

Eggs Benedict Arnold

> Ham slices
> Toast
> Tomato slice
> Poached eggs

Put ham on toast, tomato on ham, poached egg on tomato and cover with Easy Cheese Sauce.

Eggs are almost always with us. These few simple ways to use them are tasty and easy.

Eggs in Potatoes

> Baked potatoes
> Cream, butter, grated cheese
> Salt, pepper
> Eggs

Bake the potato, scoop out most of the filling while hot and mash it with butter, cream and seasoning. Put it back into the shell leaving a hollow for a raw egg. Return to oven and bake till egg is set.

Eggs in Tomatoes

> Tomatoes
> Salt, pepper, bread crumbs
> Eggs

Cut the top off large, firm tomatoes, and scoop out meat. Mix it with salt, pepper, and a few crumbs, return to shells and leave room for a raw egg. Set each tomato in a custard cup and return to oven, 400°, until egg is set.

Eggs in Stuffing

Leftover turkey or chicken stuffing
Leftover gravy
Eggs

Mix the stuffing with the gravy and spread on a shallow oven-proof dish. Make hollows with the back of a table-spoon and break a raw egg into each. Bake in the oven at 350° till the eggs are set.

Friday Specials. Bless cans!

Seafood Scramble

FOR FOUR:

1 6-ounce can, or 1 cup of crabmeat or lobster meat
1 tablespoon butter
1 teaspoon grated onion
1 teaspoon curry powder
4 eggs
3 tablespoons cream
Toast
Catsup

Pick over seafood for bones. Melt butter in skillet and blend in onions and curry powder. Add seafood and sauté for 5 minutes. Beat the eggs with the cream, pour

into the skillet, and scramble together. Serve on buttered
toast that has been covered with a thick layer of catsup.

Curried Crab

FOR TWO OR THREE:

- 1 6-ounce can crabmeat
- 1 teaspoon curry powder
- 3 black pitted olives, halved
- 1 cup cream sauce

Heat the crabmeat, curry powder and olives in the cream
sauce. Serve on rice.

Quick Crab Casserole

FOR FOUR:

- 1 6-ounce can crabmeat
- 1 can condensed mushroom soup
- ¼ cup milk
- 2 (or more) tablespoons sherry

Mix crabmeat with soup and milk, heat to boiling point,
add sherry, blend and serve on toast.

Spiced Salmon for Summer

FOR THREE OR FOUR:

- 1 cup vinegar
- 2 teaspoons mixed pickle spice
- 1 can salmon, drained

Bring vinegar to a boil with the spices, pour over fish in
a bowl and let sit overnight in icebox. Delicious drained,
with mayonnaise.

Kedgeree

(The British eat this for breakfast)

FOR FIVE:

2 cups cooked rice
2 cups canned or fresh cooked, boned fish
4 hard-boiled eggs, chopped
½ cup cream
Salt, pepper, curry powder

Mix in a casserole and heat thoroughly.

There are things in those cans that most of us never realized!

Hot Hash

FOR THREE:

1 onion, grated
1 tablespoon oil or butter
2 tablespoons mango chutney
1 teaspoon Worcestershire sauce
1 teaspoon curry powder
1 can corned beef hash

Sauté onion in fat, remove from fire and stir in seasonings. Blend in hash, put in greased casserole, and bake at 400° for 20 minutes.

Chicken Paprika

FOR TWO OR THREE:

1 onion, sliced
Butter
1 teaspoon paprika
1 can fricasseed chicken
¼ cup sour cream
Cooked noodles
Slivered almonds

Sauté the onion in butter, add the paprika and ¼ cup water. Cook until onion is soft, add chicken, heat thoroughly, stir in sour cream. Serve in a ring of noodles, sprinkled with slivered almonds.

Chicken Elégante

FOR THREE:

1 can fricasseed chicken
4 tablespoons sherry
Curry powder, pepper, salt, butter
White seedless grapes

Simmer all ingredients except the grapes together until thoroughly hot. Put in serving dish, garnish with grapes, and serve with rice.

Soup is so easy to get down when the lunch hour is so short.

Quick Ham and Pea Soup

FOR THREE OR FOUR:

1 can condensed green pea soup
1 small can deviled ham
1 can water
Celery salt

Mix well, bring to a boil and serve.

Ham and Tomato Soup

FOR THREE OR FOUR:

1 grated onion
1 tablespoon butter
1 can condensed tomato soup
1 cup canned consommé
1 chopped ripe tomato
1 small can deviled ham

Sauté onion in butter, add soups, tomato and ham. Bring to a boil, stir well and serve.

Winter Day Soup

FOR THREE:

1 can Scotch broth
1 can kidney beans (do not drain)
1 can water
2 tablespoons sherry

Mix together, simmer, add sherry just before serving.

This was contributed by one of the "first ladies" of the Army, and first with all who know her. Mrs. Maxwell Taylor gives us —

Near Pizzas

FOR SIX:

4 tablespoons grated onions
2 tablespoons olive oil
1 can tomatoes
2 tablespoons salt, or more
¾ pound yellow cheese
6 English muffins (or thick-sliced bread, in a pinch)

Cook the onion in the oil until it is soft, but not brown. Add tomatoes and salt and bring to a boil. Simmer until most of the liquid is gone. Add cheese and stir until melted, but watch it as it burns easily.

In the meantime, light the broiler: split the English muffins: toast on one side under the broiler; butter lightly when brown.

Put muffins in a large baking pan, close together, pour the sauce over them and toast until bubbly and light brown.

NOTE: The pretoasting and buttering keeps the mixture from soaking into the bread. Some families (like ours!) like chili powder added to the salt.

This is how we got the vitamins into ours, long ago. They didn't even know it was good for them!

Salad Balls

Grated raw carrots
Peanut butter
Raisins

Roll into balls, moistened with just a dab of mayonnaise, and serve on a lettuce leaf.

Candle Salad

Peeled bananas
Canned pineapple rings
Maraschino cherries
One thin slice of green pepper

Stand half a banana upright in the hole in the pineapple, fasten a cherry to the tip with toothpick, and fasten the green pepper slice to the pineapple with a toothpick to look like a handle.

Pig Salad

Hard-boiled eggs
Cloves
Toothpicks and ears cut from paper
Lettuce
Mixed frozen vegetables, cooked and chilled, and mixed with a little mayonnaise

Make tail and eyes on each "pig" with the cloves, give him toothpick legs, paper ears, and set a trough of one lettuce leaf, filled with the vegetables, in front of his nose.

Three tasty little suppers that saved many a rainy day.

Eggs Goldenrod

Hard-boiled eggs, remove the yolks and cut up the whites. Heat the whites in cream sauce, and spread on buttered toast. Put the yolks through a ricer and sprinkle on top of the creamed whites.

Baked Apples, their centers filled with raisins

Bean Fest

Fill a custard cup with canned baked beans, mixed with a teaspoon of catsup. Cut up one weenie for each cup, and put the pieces on top of the beans. Heat in oven till bubbling.

Half a tomato with a blob of mayonnaise on lettuce

Lemon Jello with white grapes set into it

Hot Summer Night

Cut cold cream of wheat into neat squares, and cover with maple syrup.

Saltines   Fresh fruit

And for a party where nobody complains about the food —

Large tray of buttered bread
Dish of peanut butter   Dish of cold cuts
Dish of jam   Dish of sliced cheese

Lettuce leaves on a large plate, each one filled with a mound of frozen mixed vegetables that have been cooked, chilled, and mixed with mayonnaise

Large bowl of vanilla ice cream
Dish of chocolate sauce
Dish of butterscotch sauce
Dish of honey
Dish of thawed frozen strawberries

But for a fancy party let's have —

Avalon Party Ice Cream

For each child, have a small real flowerpot. Line this with foil, fill it with chocolate ice cream, and sprinkle grated chocolate on top. Keep frozen until time to serve, and then put one *real* flower in each pot.

You can live without preachers
And live without books,
But civilized man cannot
Live without cooks!

Index

CPSIA information can be obtained
at www.ICGtesting.com
Printed in the USA
FFHW020116131118
49385728-53701FF